MARSHA WILSON CHALL

Happy Birthday,

AMERICA!

illustrated by GUY PORFIRIO

HarperCollinsPublishers

Cousin Jean calls first thing in the morning. "Guess what?" she says. "The corn's knee high—it's the Fourth of July!" As if we didn't know what day it is!

Dad strings up the hammock, then stakes the croquet set. Mom digs in back of the cupboard for picnic plates with three parts. I wrap my spokes in red crepe paper. Streamers shoot from my handlebars like fire.

For a whole week now I've been practicing names. I even sent my school picture to Great-aunt Lucille—last year she thought I was a guest.

Before we are ready, car doors slam. BAM, BANG, BANG, BAM!
Joe and Todd, Janie and John, Uncle Bruce and Aunt Tina swoop
over the lawn. Janie's got a curly permanent, and Todd's grown
as tall as Mom's clematis.

"How old are you now?" he asks.

"Almost nine," I tell him.

"Thought so," he says, and heads off to the horseshoe pit with
Joe. He's in the sixth grade at least.

Here comes the tub of tapioca pudding, balanced on top of Big Bill's cooler.
Great-grandma's right behind him. "Keep it steady, Bill," she says.
This year she's brought her bathing suit. "Just in case," she tells me.
In case of what, I wonder. "Great-grandma, the lake is still there."

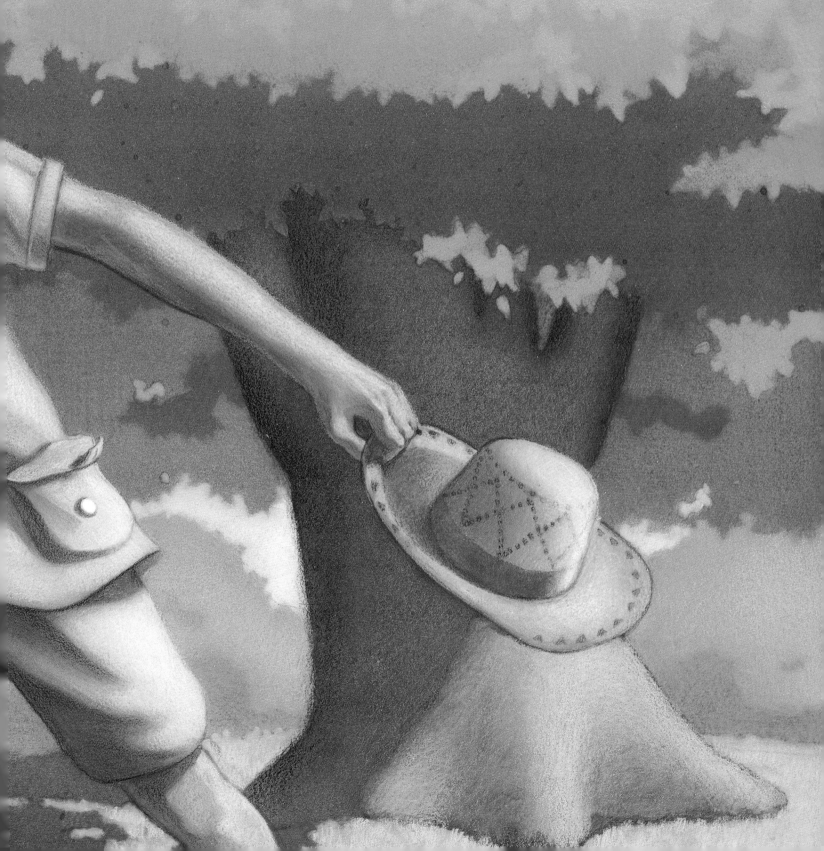

A long car winds around the corner. "Candy apple red," says Dad. "It has to be Uncle Howard." *And* Aunt Marion, *and* Uncle Kirk, *and* Great-aunt Lucille.

They squeeze me and pat me and lipstick smack me. "Candy apple cheeks," I tell Dad.

Then Uncle Kirk helps our California cousins park their motor home. From here they're driving on to Owatonna.

The twins bounce down the path, swinging bags that match their sandals.

"Hi!" "Hi!" they yell. Mary Beth's in stars. Shary Lynn's in stripes. Today I can tell them apart.

"Line up for the parade," I shout. The twins start marching. Left, right, left, right. Of course they stay in step.

"I wish I had a bike to ride." Cousin Betsy stares at mine. "I learned how this summer," she tells me.

"Mine might be too big for you," I say.

She wobbles to start, then makes two spins round the driveway.

"The parade's a lot longer," I tell her, but I give in anyway. She needs the practice.

At City Hall, the Grand Marshal,
pink as ruby grapefruit, blows the whistle.
Fire engines blare. Drums roll, *brrrmm, bmm-bmm*.
The band strikes up the "Stars and Stripes Forever."
Batons flash in the sky.

Cousin Joe pushes me in a wheelbarrow float. I'm Princess
Kay of the Milky Way, waving to both curbs of my kingdom. By
Tenth Street and Main, my crown is lopsided. My tablecloth cape
has trailed behind me for twelve blocks now. Mom will have to
use another one on the picnic table.

An army of aunts swarms out of the kitchen, carrying sweet-pickle jars and casseroles. Margie clangs the dinner bell. Merrill carves the roast beef. Todd and Janie and I race for the first place in line.

I spear strawberries and pineapple from Mom's summer bowl. It's painted like a watermelon. Then ten black olives—one for each finger.

Auntie Joyce brought her red, white, and blue Jell-O, shaped like the United States.

"It's too pretty to eat," says Great-aunt Lucille, just like she says every
year. But someone has to. I plop Florida down right next to my lasagna.

"Save Maine for me!" Cousin Tommie calls from the line. I think he
went to college there.

For dessert, it's Jan's no-nut fudge, two brownies, and blueberry pie.

"A big glass of milk?" Great-grandma asks.

"No thanks, Gram," I answer. "Lemonade, please."

After lunch we change into our swimsuits.

"Hold your horseflies," says Uncle Howard. "Let that food digest." He pats his belly. I pull mine in.

We play a game of crazy eights. He loses. I let him double-jump me in checkers.

"Strategy," he tells me.

"First one past the dock wins. Ready, set, GO!"

Last year I couldn't swim this far. The water is cold, and I can't touch bottom.

"Come back!" they shout from the end of the dock. I must be past the drop-off point. "Can you make it?"

"Sure," I yell, and back-float home.

Uncle Bud whacks off the end of a watermelon, then saws it in round slabs. We each get a half.

"Keep your seeds for the contest," Aunt Eleanor reminds us.

I eat the soft, white ones, but save the black spitters—they go the farthest.

My big cousin David works one around before cutting loose. "Never get dry," he tells me, then dips low, spits high.

Little Bill dribbles one down his chin. *Plup.* It sticks to his chest. He wins for the shortest.

Betsy twirls around before she fires.

I come in sixth place, right behind her. Next year I'll do better—work it around, never get dry, twirl, dip low, spit high.

I'm full of watermelon, but already it's time to eat again. Betsy follows me into line.

"Tapioca pudding?" Great-grandma asks. The tub is still half full.

"Thanks," I say, and slide it to the edge of my plate. "Want to eat with me, Betsy?" Her bangs shrink up when she smiles.

Uncle Howard lights fifty candles on our Fourth of July cake, our freedom cake. He sings from his belly, "Happy birthday to you...." We join in higher, "Happy birthday, America. Happy birthday to you."

"Make a wish for her," Great-grandma says.

We blow out all the candles on the first try. All our wishes will come true.

As the sun fades away, Dad announces, "It's time!" He casts off the bow lines. Auntie Joyce wraps the babies in thick towels to keep them warm. Boats flicker on the water like fireflies. The Jost family floats by. "Strawberries in yet?" asks Grandpa. "Bumper crop," says Mr. Jost.

From Powderhorn Island piccolos pipe and cymbals clash.

"Look!" I point. A ball of fire shoots up, *up*, UP . . . BOOM! then bursts into gold-and-blue sparkles.

"Oooooh," we sigh together.

"It's a spider," Todd yells.

"An octopus," says Janie.

"A chrysanthemum," Great-grandma whispers.

Ba-BANG! The sky thunders. The sound pours into the lake and laps at our boat. Baby Scott cries.

Is this the grand finale? I cover my ears and steady my eyes. Pinwheels, feathers, volcanoes and rockets, dragons and fire flakes. Our faces glow red and green and blue and gold.

Then there's only starlight. The whole lake cheers; boat horns blast.

"What did you think?" Grandpa asks, then answers himself, like always. "Best I've ever seen."

On the beach we wave our sparklers in loops and stars and figure eights.
I write my name in giant letters. It twinkles over the lake.

We hold our last sparklers up like candles, count one, two, three, then yell,
"Happy birthday, America!" across the water.

Voices call back from the other side, "Happy birthday, America!" I hear them
all around me, wishes to us, wishes to them, wishes to everyone.

To my clan, the Pecks,
and to Americans everywhere
—M.W.C.

To David
—G.P.

Watercolor paints and colored pencils
were used for the full-color illustrations.
The text type is 13-point Veljovic Medium

Happy Birthday, America!
Text copyright © 2000 by Marsha Wilson Chall
Illustrations copyright © 2000 by Guy Porfirio
Printed in Singapore at Tien Wah Press. All rights reserved.
http://www.harperchildrens.com

LIBRARY OF CONGRESS CATALOGING-IN-PUBLICATION DATA
Chall, Marsha Wilson.
Happy birthday, America!/by Marsha Wilson Chall; illustrated by Guy Porfirio.
p. cm.
Summary: Joined by an army of aunts, uncles, and cousins,
eight-year-old Kay and her family celebrate the Fourth of July.
ISBN 0-688-13051-8 (trade)—ISBN 0-688-13052-6 (library)
[1. Fourth of July—Fiction. 2. Family life—Fiction.] I. Porfirio, Guy, ill. II. Title.
PZ7.C3496 Hap 2000   J FIC 1-3
[E]—dc20
                                        93-049820

3 5 7 9 10 8 6 4
❖